Hamster Holmes

A BIG-TIME PUZZLE

By **Albin Sadar**
Illustrated by **Valerio Fabbretti**

Ready-to-Read

Simon Spotlight

New York London Toronto Sydney New Delhi

For

..-. .- -- .. ..-. -.--

—A. S.

To my parents, Daniela and Marco
—V. F.

SIMON SPOTLIGHT
An imprint of Simon & Schuster Children's Publishing Division
1230 Avenue of the Americas, New York, New York 10020
This Simon Spotlight edition December 2019
Text copyright © 2019 by Albin Sadar
Illustrations copyright © 2015, 2019 by Valerio Fabbretti
All rights reserved, including the right of reproduction in whole or in part in any form.
SIMON SPOTLIGHT, READY-TO-READ, and colophon are registered trademarks of
Simon & Schuster, Inc.
For information about special discounts for bulk purchases, please contact Simon & Schuster
Special Sales at 1-866-506-1949 or business@simonandschuster.com.
Manufactured in the United States of America 1119 LAK
10 9 8 7 6 5 4 3 2 1
Library of Congress Cataloging-in-Publication Data I Names: Sadar, Albin, author. I Fabbretti, Valerio,
illustrator. Title: Hamster Holmes, a big-time puzzle / by Albin Sadar ; illustrated by Valerio Fabbretti.
Other titles: Big-time puzzle Description: First Simon Spotlight edition. I New York : Simon Spotlight,
[2019] I Series: Hamster Holmes ; [book 6] I Audience: Ages 5-7. I Audience: Grades K-1. I Summary:
"Hamster Holmes and his firefly sidekick, Dr. Watt, . . . are enjoying a fair when a friend invites them
to race to find a hidden hourglass. Can they solve the word puzzles in time? Time will tell!"–Provided
by publisher. Includes facts and activities. Identifiers: LCCN 2019029170 I ISBN 9781534421974
(paperback) I ISBN 9781534421981 (hardcover) ISBN 9781534421998 (eBook) Subjects: CYAC:
Mystery and detective stories. I Word games–Fiction. I Hamsters–Fiction. I Animals–Fiction.
Classification: LCC PZ7.1.S23 Haf 2019 I DDC [E]–dc23

Hamster Holmes and his
firefly friend, Dr. Watt,
loved solving mysteries.
Today they took a break at
a fair in the park.
They played games and ate treats.

Then they saw their old friends,
a big fly named Horsey
and Gary the gumshoe gopher,
who were also detectives.
Dr. Watt said hello.
He used Morse code
to get his point across.

He blinked his light on and off
to form the dashes and dots.
A short flash of light was a dot.
A long flash of light was a dash.
Horsey said hello by making
a loud buzzing noise.

A ·–   J ·–––   S ···
B –···   K –·–   T –
C –·–·   L ·–··   U ··–
D –··   M ––   V ···–
E ·   N –·   W ·––
F ··–·   O –––   X –··–
G ––·   P ·––·   Y –·––
H ····   Q ––·–   Z ––··
I ··   R ·–·

They were all catching up when
Ouchy the porcupine walked up.
"Hello to my favorite detectives!
I am holding a contest today,
and you are just in time to
be a part of it," he said.

"It is a race to find the answers to four clues. Each answer leads you to the next clue. The last clue leads you to the prize!"

Ouchy went on.
"The first team to find all
the answers wins this hourglass
filled with real gold dust!"
An hourglass is a special clear
container that usually holds sand.

It is used to measure a minute,
hour, or other amount of time.
When all the gold dust
flows from the top to the
bottom of this hourglass,
it means an hour has passed.

"Do you want to play?"
asked Ouchy.
"I am up for it,"
said Hamster Holmes.
Dr. Watt blinked an answer.
Horsey and Gary decided
to play too.

Ouchy smiled and looked at his
pocket watch. Then he told them
the first clue.
"You can run, walk, or fly
to this wheel, but even though
it spins around it does not
go anywhere."

"It must be that prize wheel
we saw at the fair,"
Gary said to Horsey.
"If we are right, the next clue
will be there."
Dr. Watt and Hamster Holmes
did not think that was the
right answer.

Gary and Horsey rushed to the
prize wheel but did not find
the next clue.

Hamster Holmes told Dr. Watt,
"I think the answer has to do
with the words run, walk, or fly."
Then Dr. Watt figured it out!

It was the running wheel!
Hamster Holmes read the
next clue aloud as Gary and
Horsey arrived.
He said,
"Do not let this next clue
stump you . . . even if you have
to dig deep for the answer."
Gary whispered something to
Horsey, and they left.

Hamster Holmes and Dr. Watt
did not know the answer.
Then Dr. Watt spotted a
tree stump nearby.
"It is a good thought,"
Hamster Holmes said,
"but I do not see the next clue,
so it must not be the right stump."

Then Dr. Watt remembered
their friend Dougie the mole
had dug his house under a
a tree stump.
"Good idea,"
said Hamster Holmes.
"It must be at his house!"

Sure enough, when they
reached Dougie's house,
they found the next clue . . .
and Gary and Horsey!
Gary read the clue aloud.
"It has hands and a face,
but it can only tell you
one thing."

"What could that mean?"
Hamster Holmes asked.
"No idea," said Gary.
"What can only tell us one
thing instead of many things?"
Hamster Holmes wondered.
Then he and Dr. Watt realized
it was a . . .

. . . clock!

Hamster Holmes and Dr. Watt
raced to the clock tower.
"The round part of a clock
is called the face, and the
long thin parts that point
at numbers are called hands.
It can tell only one thing,
which is time!"
said Hamster Holmes.

Dr. Watt found the last clue
in front of the clock on a sundial,
which tells time using shadows.
Hamster Holmes read the clue aloud.
"If you open the right door,
you will be the winner!" he said.

"But how do we know which
door is the right one?"
asked Gary, who was just steps
behind them.
"Is it the door on the left,
the door in the middle,
or the door on the right?"

"This mystery is . . . solved!"
said Hamster Holmes.
"The door on the RIGHT is
the correct door!"

When he opened the door,
Ouchy was there!
Ouchy handed the hourglass to
Hamster Holmes and Dr. Watt.
"It was a big puzzle, but you
solved it in record time!"

"Good job," said Gary.
"Good game,"
said Hamster Holmes.
"We would like to have you all
over for snack time tomorrow to
thank you for a fun time!"

The next day, Hamster Holmes put
the hourglass in a place of honor.
Then they all sat down for snacks
and shared their favorite mysteries.
It was the perfect end to a
great adventure!

Do you want to
solve mysteries like
Hamster Holmes and Dr. Watt?
Turn the page for fun activities, a
special case to solve
with Morse code, and more!

Time for a Game!

There are four different timepieces shown in this story. A timepiece is something that is used to find out the time of day or to measure time.

Use a pencil or crayon to draw a line from each name to the matching timepiece:

clock tower

pocket watch

hourglass

sundial

When you're done, look in the answer key on the last page of this book to find out if you matched the words and pictures correctly . . . and see if you can find these four timepieces in the story, too!

Solve the Mystery!

What is Dr. Watt saying in Morse code? It is a mystery . . . but maybe you can help solve it.

Check the answer key on the last page of this book when you are ready. You can also use the Morse code chart to write a message to a friend!

Find the Missing Words

Hamster Holmes loves books, reading, and everything about words. He also loves puzzles, but this one has him stumped. Can you help him find the words in this word jumble? Keep in mind that words can go from side to side or top to bottom.

GOPHER

CLOCK

WHEEL

DETECTIVE

FAIR

H	Z	G	R	D	D	J
Y	F	W	R	C	E	A
X	F	A	I	R	T	Y
W	G	O	P	H	E	R
H	P	A	F	C	C	N
E	C	Y	K	L	T	N
E	K	H	J	O	I	H
L	V	D	L	C	V	V
F	W	Z	V	K	E	A

Great job, detective!

When you're done, you can check the answer
key at the end of this book.

A Mystery in a Work of Art

Did you know that detectives like Hamster Holmes and Dr. Watt can help solve art mysteries, too?

Believe it or not, one of the tools they use to solve this kind of mystery is an X-ray machine! The same kind of machine that lets doctors look at your bones is sometimes used to look underneath layers of paint on a canvas at what is called "underpainting." An X-ray machine can help show if there are other, older paintings underneath.

This technology has been used to solve many art mysteries. Sometimes people think a painting is lost forever . . . but it turns out the artist just painted over it!

Why would artists paint over their work? It depends, but sometimes it is because they didn't like the original painting, and sometimes it is because they don't have enough money to buy a new canvas so they reuse an old one. With the help of X-rays and other technology, art mysteries can be . . . solved!

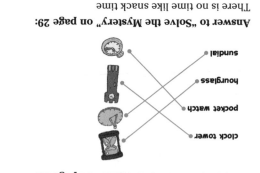